CAT MESSAGE

A LOCKDOWN LOVE STORY

C J HARRISON

Published in 2021
by Great Escape Publishing.

chrisseyharrison.com

A CIP catalogue record of this book is available from the British Library.

ISBN 978-0-9575336-8-4
eBook available - ISBN 978-0-9575336-7-7

Printed and Distributed by Ingramspark.

Cover design and typeset by Chrissey Harrison
using graphic assets licensed from Shutterstock.

Cat Message

A Lockdown Love Story

C J Harrison

Cat Message

A Lockdown Love Story

C J Harrison

28th March 2020

Somewhere in the suburbs of Milton Keynes

Day 9 of Self-isolation

It's raining, and I've just used up the last of the proper milk. Even if the shops had milk, I'm not supposed to go out. I'm one of the "at-risk" people all this social distancing is supposed to protect. For me, it's my asthma.

And the cancer. Can't forget that. I had twenty-five per cent of my left lung removed five years ago, followed by a round of chemo. They caught it extremely early and so far, so good, but the last thing I want to do is prod my cancer-susceptible lungs with Covid-19.

Sitting at my kitchen table, I sip my tea (my last decent cup in who knows how long), stare at the rain streaking down the French doors, and try to decide what to do with my day. I have a stack of commissions to work on, and you'd think being quarantined would improve my productivity, but it's having the opposite effect. It's all I can think about. How bad things are out there. How much worse they're going to get. Whether my parents are listening to my sister and staying home like they're supposed to. How much food I have left in the house. When I should start rationing the bog roll.

I *should* be better at this. I'm nearly forty, and I'm pretty sure I'm supposed to have my shit together by now. Feels more like I've been going backwards since I split with my ex-girlfriend. The cancer may not have stamped my ticket (yet), but my relationship didn't survive it.

Actually, to be fair, this last year I had started to turn things around. I was making a decent living freelancing, enough that I'd invested in a studio at a co-working place in town. Through there I'd met Lydia, who I thought might, maybe, be interested in me. Life was looking up.

Now I'm not even allowed to go to the shops.

I'm supposed to rely on friends and family to deliver things I need, but my family are miles away, and I don't feel comfortable asking friends. Not until things get desperate, at least. Switching from semi-skimmed to long-life oat milk is not desperate.

Things could be worse. At least I have plenty of space here, especially with the garden. I'm so glad my ex and I bought when we could, even though it didn't last between us. There's no way I'd be able to get a new mortgage now.

And I'm not completely alone; Tawny is sitting on the mat by the doors, glaring at the rain like it's a personal insult. She keeps me company. When she's not out adventuring. I'm jealous of her freedom and the fact that she has nothing to worry about so long as I keep feeding her. I have loads of cat food. I'm more likely to run out of human food and be forced to share her rations than the other way around. Litter might become a problem, but she's fairly good at using the "outdoor litter box", otherwise known as next door's veg beds.

Shame that's not a solution for me and my bog roll problem.

I chuckle to myself at the thought of taking a shit in Carol and Stu's immaculate garden. Imagine the looks on their faces. The stupidest things are making me laugh. It's the lack of human contact slowly wearing away my sanity.

It's only been nine days! I don't know why I'm finding this so hard. I'm used to working from home, managing my time, being on my own. It should be easy.

One thing at a time. I'm going to savour this cup of tea. I'm not going to let it go cold while I'm distracted by work or whatever, I'm going to taste every mouthful and enjoy it. It's a damn good cup of tea.

Day 10

I'm working on a digital painting. One of my commissions. This one is for a sci-fi comic book cover. I do plenty of sequential art, but there is something particularly satisfying about the concentrated effort and reward of a more detailed and polished single piece. Or, normally there is. At the moment, I'm struggling to find the focus for a sustained effort.

Tawny saunters in and sniffs her way around her office, checking it's all still hers, which it is. Once she's satisfied, she jumps up on the desk, walks on the keyboard and headbutts my hand, causing me to scrawl a line across the tablet. I lift her into my lap and ctrl+z the damage.

Tawny is nearly two. She still has the sleek, slightly kittenish shape of a cat that hasn't filled out yet. I've had her since she was three months old. She was the last of a litter to be adopted. The volunteers at the shelter said she was nervous around kids and that tortoiseshells like her are sometimes harder to rehome because they're "ugly" (apparently). I think she looks like a sunny autumn day, and she gave me cuddles when we met – I'm a sucker for anyone who shows me affection.

The volunteers also expressed how unusual it is for a single man to adopt a cat. I said I was trying to challenge the gender stereotype of the cat lady – to show that an eccentric, lonely, unloved (un-loveable?) man could just as easily fill the void in his life with feline companionship as could a woman. My speech did not go down well, but they still let me have her.

She rubs her chin on my arm and something snags against my sleeve. There's a small plastic tube taped to her collar. My isolation-addled brain is baffled as to how it could have got there until I remember there are still other humans in the world.

"What's this?" I ask. I'm not expecting the cat to answer. Talking to pets is a normal thing that people do. It's perfectly normal.

The edge of a piece of paper pokes out the end and, pinning the cat with one arm, I extract it. Tawny, slightly miffed, wriggles out of my grasp and gets down.

It's a note: *Whose cat is this? It keeps coming into my house.*

I've still been in contact with the outside world – I'm not on a desert island for God's sake – but it's mostly been via email, text chat or phone. Interacting with the world through a glass screen. Somehow, this is different. It's *real*. Someone touched this paper and wrote this note, and now I'm holding it in my hand, and it's like I'm touching them by proxy.

That came out wrong.

How is it possible to feel embarrassed *on your own*?

Tawny is staring at me.

"Are you waiting for me to write back?" If Tawny's been trespassing regularly enough for the mystery neighbour to enquire by collar message, she's bound to go back. It might be fun to see if my message reaches them. God knows I could use a little fun. Tawny's response is to wash her face with a paw and yawn. I'm not sure how to interpret that.

I'm going to do it. Why not?

I take a square of yellow paper from the note block on my desk and write:

Hello. She's mine, so far as anyone can ever actually "own" a cat. Her name is Tawny, my name is Nick. Who are you?

I roll my message up, slide off my chair and snag Tawny before she can flee. I pop the message in the holder. "Go on then, deliver it." I release her, and she darts out of the room, clearly deciding I am "being weird".

Day 11

Tawny went out and came back in a few times yesterday, but only to mooch around the garden. The yellow paper in the tube stayed put. This morning she was out for a long time, and she's just returned through her catflap into the kitchen. I drop what I'm doing (laundry) because the yellow paper is gone. There's white paper in the tube now.

I sit on the floor. Tawny, eager for a fuss, trots over. "Hey, little postman. Is that a letter for me?"

"Mraaow."

I surreptitiously extract the new message while distracting her with scritches. Unrolling it, I read:

Hello, Nick. I'm Amanda. Tawny naps in my conservatory. I don't mind if you don't. Just thought you should know.

Amanda. My mystery collar messager has a name.

"Would it be weird if I wrote back?" I ask the cat. She twists to nibble an itch at the base of her tail and then dismisses me in favour of a drink from her water fountain. I take this to mean she doesn't have an opinion on the matter.

It's silly. I don't even know who Amanda is – except that she was curious and ingenious enough to think of taping a tube to Tawny's collar in the first place – but watching the cat, to see when my message disappeared and a new reply took its place, has been the highlight of my week.

I tend to think of myself as an introvert, but I need the unexpected little twists and turns of life that come from other people. Right now, I'm trapped in a bubble. Outside, the world is on fire and there's bugger all I can do, but inside, nothing happens unless I make it happen. It's messing with my head. I need this little distraction to mix things up. Add a little unpredictability to my day.

"Just thought you should know" sounds like the end of a conversation. A dismissal. "I don't mind if you don't" on the other hand is a kind of question. What if I did mind? Then I'd have to write back. I mean, I *don't* mind, but Amanda doesn't know that.

I pop upstairs to my office. At my desk, I select another yellow square from my note block and ponder what I could say to keep this little game, this little distraction, going. I want to know more about Amanda. Is she an adult, a child, living alone or with her family?

Tawny follows after a few minutes, doing another circuit to check everything is still hers.

Perhaps I can prompt Amanda to offer some insight about herself by offering something about myself first. Something relevant to the situation we're all in together right now. I write, keeping my handwriting small so I can fit more on:

Hi Amanda, If you don't mind, I don't mind. Tawny has the luxury of being able to visit and socialise. As someone who has to self-isolate, I cannot begrudge her that. I haven't left the house in 10 days. You?

I sign it with my initial. *N.*

My courier sauntered out of the room while I was agonising over my wording. I go looking for her.

Day 12

This morning I learn that Amanda is also self-isolating due to having had a transplant and being on immunosuppressants. She hasn't left her house in two weeks, but her parents drop round supplies every few days.

Now I'm building a picture of who Amanda might be. I guess she's somewhere between twenty-five and forty – if she's relying on her parents then, one, she doesn't live with them and, two, they must be younger than seventy themselves. She probably doesn't have grown-up kids to call on, but it's possible she could have young ones. Or she might live alone; if she lived with a husband or partner, they could run errands.

It's all guesses.

I know she likes cats but doesn't have one of her own, since I don't think Tawny would feel safe napping in another cat's territory.

I watched Tawny out my office window earlier to see where she went, and I'm pretty sure Amanda's house is somewhere to the left. Obviously not next door, or the house two down; I know my neighbours there. I'm thinking she might live on the street parallel to mine. There's a footpath that the gardens on both streets back onto. People come and go that way via their garden gates, but only if they're walking. I count the houses. I think the one directly behind mine is number 12 on that street, so Amanda's would be an even number higher than 12.

There are too many shrubs and trees blocking the view to see which houses have conservatories. And besides, I'm curious, but I don't want to slip into creepy stalker behaviour.

Her latest message asks why I am self-isolating. She wouldn't include questions if she didn't expect me to write back, would she?

I explain about my asthma and the cancer. It's weird putting it in writing. I'm a cancer "survivor". I am in "remission", a word I hate because it sounds so temporary; I'm not cured, I'm just not sick right now. It makes me feel like I'm living on borrowed time, and I am shit scared that coronavirus could speed up my clock. My doctors have said the chances of the cancer returning are low. But, their definition of low is a long way from zero, and I have to live the rest of my life with odds I definitely wouldn't stake my life savings on (four in five I stay cancer-free if you're wondering).

Obviously, I don't put all of that in my note to Amanda, only the basics.

I do make space to lament my dwindling supply of bog roll and that oat milk is just not the same, trying to keep it light. I ask if she is working from home.

The pieces of paper are small, but so long as there is an unanswered question, I can hope this will keep going. Chatting to clients, friends, family and so on is one thing, but there's a different kind of satisfaction to be gained from meeting someone new.

Day 13

When Tawny returns from her morning nap at Amanda's, there is something bulky attached to her collar, and she is not happy about it. It's attached with rubber bands, and no matter how much she scratches, it's not coming off.

It's a packet of tissues, one of those pocket pouches you get with 10 tissues in for blowing your nose when you're out and about. It comes with a message:

In case of emergency. I'm furloughed from my job at the arts centre. I'm the Event Space Co-ordinator, which is a fancy name for a person in charge of a diary and a set of keys. You?

I'm starting to like Amanda.

Day 14

More rain today, and Tawny has decided she'd rather take her morning nap on my bed instead of in Amanda's conservatory. My postman is sleeping on the job because it's raining. The cheek! But she's so cute I can't stay mad at her. It just means I'm going to have to wait another day for the next piece in my Amanda puzzle.

Meanwhile, the latest in the saga of Nick's dwindling household supplies – I'm out of Just for Men hair dye. Hey, don't judge me, lots of men use it. It's only to cover a few greys; I noticed this morning while I was shaving that they're starting to show where my roots are growing out. I'm trying to resist the urge to count them or pluck them out. What does it matter? It's not like anyone is going to see.

I guess it just makes me feel old, which in turn makes me think about what I'm missing out on because of this bastard pandemic. It's stealing months, perhaps even a year of my life. Worse, it's stealing from the last two years of my *thirties,* which means it's stealing time I was hoping to use to find someone to settle down with. Someone to start a family with, late in my life as it would be. I still want all that, but somehow the big four zero feels like an expiry date. A cutoff.

Logically, I know it's not that arbitrary, but I also don't know how long I have with those low-but-not-zero odds of the cancer returning. The older I get, the fewer chances I'll have. Can you blame me for wanting to hide the physical reminders of that?

Day 16

I am officially hitting desperate, says the man eating a tin of expired broccoli and stilton soup with half a dozen Jacob's cream crackers for lunch. I'm either going to have to go to the shops or call someone for a favour. I'm not *supposed* to go to the shops. I don't *want* to ask for a favour.

I expressed this dilemma to Amanda in yesterday's cat message. Tawny only ever seems to visit once a day (or not at all if it's raining), so we're limited to one exchange. It's frustratingly not enough for me. I want to talk to my new friend and get to know her. She's the only other "at-risk" person I know, and I want to share the fear, the loneliness, the frustration. I want to talk about how helpless I feel having to depend on other people. I want to know if she's finding it as hard as I am and whether she's struggling with the same things or different things.

Tawny interrupts my soup and crackers (which is good, because it's not sitting well and I'm not sure I want the rest). She has a new note.

Amanda says to stop being such a MAN and ask someone for help, and now I feel like I've been told off by my mum. Well, not *my* mum, who hates being a bother to anyone and would more likely sympathise with my situation than tell me off, but you get what I mean – it's an effective kick up the backside.

I call my mate, Dave. He lives closest, and so I figure he'd be the least inconvenienced. He's keen to help, and we agree for me to email him a shopping list for a week of supplies, which he'll drop off in my garden shed tomorrow afternoon (Sunday).

We chat for almost an hour about how crazy everything is in the world right now. It feels good to talk out loud. Most of my conversations recently have been in text form. Verbally, I've probably said more to Tawny than any human in the last two weeks.

Dave's worried about his job. He works at an ad agency and, while he can work from home, a lot of their clients are scaling back their marketing budgets. He's worried the business will struggle, and he's not sure what that will mean.

I almost envy him; I have only myself to blame for my work problems. I'm falling behind on my deadlines, even though I have unlimited time and no other commitments. My sleep patterns are all screwed up, which is making me drowsy and sapping my energy. My motivation and focus are just gone half the time.

I feel like I'm failing at all this for no reason. Even the little things like showering and doing the dishes. I keep forgetting to hang the laundry that's been sat in my machine for three days, and I don't know why. I'm not usually like this, but everything feels ten times more difficult than it should.

After I get off the phone with Dave, I thank Amanda for her advice, tell her I made arrangements, and ask how she's doing. At least I've addressed one problem today.

Now I'm going to sit at my desk, for not less than a solid hour, and try to get some work done.

DAY 20

Amanda had to go to the hospital on Monday. She didn't say why in Sunday's note, except that it wasn't Covid related. I think she only told me to explain why there wouldn't be a message on Monday and that there might not be a message on Tuesday if they kept her in. It surprised me that she would share something so personal with, effectively, a stranger, but I was grateful she did. I'm not sure how I would have felt if Tawny had come home empty-handed (empty-pawed?) and I hadn't known why. Amanda doesn't feel like a stranger to me anymore. She feels like someone I know at least well enough to meet up for a coffee and a chat.

As it was, a message did come Tuesday, yesterday, with no further mention of her hospital visit. I didn't pry.

Right now, I'm standing by the open patio doors, enjoying a bit of fresh air after a workout. That's right, I did some exercise today. I regret having been so lazy over the last couple of weeks though because now my asthma is flaring up. I take another puff on my inhaler and hold it in. Despite the tightness in my chest, I feel better for having worked up a sweat.

I'm supposed to go outside to get daily exercise. *Daily!* Bollocks to that. I never exercised outside before the pandemic; I'm not going to take up jogging now. I'll stick with my half an hour on my exercise bike and a few push-ups and sit-ups, thank you.

Tawny returned a few minutes ago, and I'm holding today's message from Amanda.

> *Nick, what do you miss most? I miss my yoga class. It's not the same on my own. A lot of things are not the same on my own. I'm tired of all this and it's only just getting started.*
>
> *– A*

It's the first time she's sounded downbeat, and it makes my chest tighten in a way I don't think the inhaler will help with.

One of the reasons I'm still standing here, holding the message, is because I'm experiencing a dreadful urge to send her my phone number. I want to know that she's okay. I want to tell her she's not alone. But, if she'd wanted to exchange personal info, she would have suggested it already. I'm sure she'd rather keep this anonymous. For now, at least.

I'm going to stand here until the urge passes.

Day 21

I am standing on my front doorstep, clapping for the NHS, and I'm not sure how I feel about it.

I wave to Stu and Carol standing on their doorstep at number 11 next door.

"Hi, Nick. How's things?" Stu calls.

"Oh, not too bad, not too bad."

"Strange times, huh?"

"Yeah." I smile and nod. That's about as many words as we've exchanged all year. I've always had the impression Stu and Carol don't like me. I know they don't like Tawny, but I think it's more than just frustration over cat poop. They don't like the fact I'm single (there must be a reason my ex left), that I don't have a "proper" job (it's not normal for a grown man to be interested in comics), and that I don't maintain my garden to their standards (I'm not sure the Royal Horticultural Society could measure up). It's fine because we ignore each other most of the time, but this pandemic is making everyone play nice.

They wave to the Pakistani family across the street at number 10 as if they are friends. The kids have drawn rainbows to put in the window and are banging wooden spoons on saucepans. Carol complained to the council once about the kids using chalk on the pavement. Some council person came and jet washed away their hopscotch and unicorns as if it were graffiti, so I bought them some more chalk, and we turned a whole section of the street into a Spiderman comic. We got our picture in the local paper.

That might be another reason Carol doesn't like me.

We clap.

It's all so disingenuous, and I hate it. I'm pretty sure all the nurses and doctors are working hard because it's their job and they're good people, not because they expect praise. I'm also pretty sure they would prefer adequate funding and PPE rather than applause, but hey ho. As soon as I deem it socially acceptable, I retreat inside.

I wonder if Amanda is clapping on her street. I think she would clap because she'd see the positive side of it. The value of community spirit. She's not a cynic like me.

Day 22

Amanda has been practising her knitting. I know this because Tawny came home wearing a miniature scarf. It's rainbow coloured and smells nice.

She also challenged me to a game of Hangman. I guessed "E", as is tradition.

DAY 24

Dave has just dropped my latest lot of groceries in the shed. We're having a sort of chat through the open French doors, and I feel a little like I'm breaking the rules.

We talk about the pandemic because that's the universal topic of conversation right now. It's nice catching up. I know Dave from uni; we both studied art and design at Reading. I have a few friends like him – mates I was close to but who drifted away when they got married, had families. It was easier when I was still with my ex because we could join in as a couple. Now I'm their single guy friend who doesn't fit into their lives.

He tells me he's struggling to juggle work with home-schooling his kids. His wife is still working her part-time job at the supermarket, but they've increased her hours to deal with the extra pressure, the cleaning, and the social distancing measures. He looks tired, his normally tanned skin pale and his beard scruffy. I feel bad about making demands on his time.

"The kids have been a handful," he says, wearily. "They miss their friends, and they're bored to pieces, so they're acting up more."

I nod my sympathy, but I'm more jealous than anything. Jealous of family in general but also of the kids specifically. I can't help but dwell on the fact I don't have any of my own and probably never will.

"I mean, it's tough on both of us," he says. "We're both so exhausted all the time, and we haven't... well, you know... since all this started."

I scoff, thinking that a dry spell with his wife is so far down in the grand scheme of problems in the world right now. "At least you're together." I immediately feel like a dick for being so insensitive.

"Ahh, sorry mate. I wasn't thinking. You haven't heard from what's-her-name then?"

It takes me a moment to twig who he's referring to. "Who? Lydia? Nah, not really."

"Did you call her?"

"I texted her. Said maybe we should leave it till things settle down. She said that sounded sensible."

Dave rolls his eyes. "Well of course she did. If you can't even make the effort to call her to tell her you don't want to make an effort, she's definitely going to assume you're not really interested."

"It wasn't like we were officially dating or anything. We only went for one drink. I just thought... I didn't want to make things complicated for her."

Dave gives me a look of exasperated pity. "Mate, you're never going to find a girlfriend if you keep thinking of yourself as an inconvenience."

I cringe. This whole conversation is making me feel guilty because the truth is I haven't thought about Lydia in weeks. I *am* lonely, but I don't miss *her*. I think I realised when everything kicked off that we weren't right for each other anyway. Our one drinks date had been pleasant enough, but she'd seemed, well, more conceited than I'd thought she'd be. Kind of judgemental. It was a bit of a relief when she agreed not to bother.

I find myself toying with the idea of telling Dave about Amanda, but I don't think he'd understand. I'm not sure *I* understand. I'm not sure how to explain that the best part of my day involves sending a woman I've never met my next guess in the game of Hangman we're playing via my cat.

"Anyway, I'd better be getting back," Dave says.

"We should get together for a pint after all this."

"Yeah, definitely," I agree, although I can't see far enough ahead to picture it happening.

"Take care, mate. Stay safe." He starts for the side gate. I wave him off and shut the patio door. I'll bring the groceries in later and PayPal what I owe him.

DAY 27

Hey Nick, I know you're on your own over there at the moment, but do you have someone special you're separated from? A girlfriend? Someone you fancy? I never realised how being alone in this house every day would make me so aware of how little space I take up. It's nice when Tawny visits.

– A

No, no one. I don't think that's in my future anymore and, honestly, I'm starting to make peace with it. At least Tawny loves me… so long as I feed her. What about you?

– N

Day 28

Last week, Amanda asked me what I missed most. At the time, I said I missed my studio, which wasn't an outright lie. I do miss it. I'm sure I'd be getting a lot more done with my proper workspace around me to keep me motivated and inspired.

But it's not what I miss *most*.

It took me a few days to work out what I missed most, but I've finally decided it's spontaneity, the whole general concept of it. I miss deciding mid-morning that I fancy a coffee, throwing on my coat and walking to Starbucks. I miss deciding at six in the evening to go see a movie. I miss bumping into a mate in town at lunchtime and arranging to go for a game of pool and a burger after work.

I think I need it as an outlet. Without it, I dwell on all the things I can't do, and, like an itch I can't scratch, it leaves me irritable and distracted.

I'm pissed off with myself today. All of my procrastination and faffing has finally caught up with me, and one of my clients has pulled their commission. Not just any client but a major publisher, and not just any commission but the £600 sci-fi cover art painting I was planning to pay my mortgage with next month. They say they're pulling the whole project because of pandemic-based "uncertainty", but they could just be saying that so they can cut me loose and find someone more reliable. They've paid me twenty per cent of what we'd agreed, and I'm left with a half-finished piece of artwork I can't do anything with. It's my own stupid fault. It was in the terms and conditions I agreed to, and if I'd delivered on time, they would have had to pay me, pandemic or no.

I'm disappointed with myself. I'm miserable. I want a beer. Actually, I want six, but I don't think I deserve any, so instead, I'm sorting my recycling, mowing the lawn, and doing a bunch of other mindless tasks I've been putting off as a kind of penance. I don't deserve to feel sorry for myself; I'm just being lazy and selfish and need to pull myself together.

I toss a glass jar into the box, and it shatters. "Bollocks!"

I suddenly realise Tawny is cowering by the shed, watching me and all the noise I'm making like she wants to make a run for her cat flap, but I'm in the way and being scary.

I stop what I'm doing, pop inside to fetch her treats and a toy then sit on the grass. I call her over. She creeps out from her hiding place as if she doesn't know me. I get it. I don't feel like I know myself right now either.

"I'm sorry, little'un. Do you want some Dreamies?" I shake the packet.

She has a couple of treats, and then I trail her feather toy on a string across the grass. Her little predator eyes dilate, and I think I am forgiven. For a little while, I let everything else fade away and play with my cat. I may not deserve fun and games, but she does. She has been perfect.

When she runs out of energy, or inclination, or patience, whichever it is, she flops on her side, and I realise there's a new message from Amanda. I retrieve it and lie down beside her.

I hesitate to unroll the paper. Like with the beer, I don't feel I deserve this little comfort right now.

Lying on my back on the fresh-cut grass, the damp penetrates my clothes. I'm done right now. I want to get off this ride. Adulthood is overrated. Adulthood is desperately wanting to go home then realising you're already there and you can't escape what's making you scared or sad.

I open the message.

*Hey, Nick. I can hear you clattering around over there. I hope you're okay, but it's okay if you're not. No one is expecting you to be at your best right now. P.S. Nice shorts. Nice legs for that matter *wink*.*

My head jerks up. She can see me? There's me worrying about my stalkerish behaviour, and she's spying on me! And flirting, maybe? Is that what this is? I suddenly feel very exposed. But, in a nice way. She lives in one of the houses that overlooks my garden then; one of the windows I can see from here is hers. I wonder if she's watching me right now? I kind of like the idea that she might be. Like she's looking out for me. Like… like maybe she cares about me. Was that why she asked if I had someone yesterday?

No one is expecting me to be at my best. Too right. Being angry with myself isn't going to solve anything;

it's just making me miserable. Maybe I'm aiming too high and being too hard on myself. I'm going to finish these chores, then I'm going to eat something healthy, chill for a bit, have a shower and go to bed early. I might even have that beer.

Tomorrow, I'm going to get my head on straight.

DAY 29

I'm worried I'm masturbating too much. TMI, I know, but it's playing on my mind.

I mean, it's a thing people do, a perfectly normal part of life, and before all this, I'd indulge two or three times a week. About a week into lockdown it began to creep up, and I did start to think about why that was – whether it was boredom or loneliness. This last week though, I've found myself doing it every day, sometimes even twice, and for longer, and I think there's a term for that: self-soothing. It's comforting, and I'm doing it because I feel so miserable.

Do I feel *ashamed?* Not really. It's 2020, and I think it's high time we get over the stigma around self-love. It's a natural thing to do, and it feels good. There are even studies saying it helps prevent prostate cancer and, having had the lung version, that is something I am fully on board with. It's not the wanking itself I'm worried about so much as how it fits into this overall pattern of unhealthy behaviour I've fallen into recently.

I'm worried I'm getting addicted or using it as a crutch.

I'm not going to stop; I'm just going to ration myself a bit. Everything in moderation, right?

This is one thing that will definitely not be going in my messages to Amanda. New promise – there will be no mention of penises!

Day 30

Hey Nick, I bought one of your comics. The first one with the space whales. You're so talented. Page 6 alone is a masterpiece. Maybe you could sign it for me when this is all over?

– A

Hey Amanda, Photon League? Oh no. Look, I can explain about the giant wang on page 6. It was a typo in the script! And then the writer wanted to keep it. Not my fault!

– N

I don't know, you make a promise not to mention penises, and somehow penises come up anyway. FML.

Just to make things abundantly clear, *Photon League* is an adult comic for adults and has sex, nudity and gore elsewhere in the script, so it was an easy mistake to make. I did not, and I cannot stress this enough, slip a cock drawing into a kids' comic book.

Just so we're clear on that.

DAY 31

Another week, another grocery delivery from Dave. He has the kids with him this time. Twelve-year-old Leon and nine-year-old Mia. They're playing with Tawny in the garden while we have a catch-up.

"Sometimes I just need to get them out of the house so Chelle can catch her breath, you know?" he says.

I set a cup of tea on the patio table then retreat inside. We're breaking the rules a tad, but I don't give a shit. The least he deserves is a cup of tea for his trouble. I'll wash my hands after.

"How's work?" I ask. I still regret the way I spoke to him last time, and I want him to know I do care about what he's going through. His struggles may be different to the ones I'm having, but they are equally valid.

"They furloughed a bunch of us. Which is okay by me if it means I keep my job."

"That's good then."

"Yeah." He glances at the kids who are fighting over Tawny's feather toy. "If you can't share, I'll take it away." They appear to work out a turn system.

Dave turns his attention back to me. "Am I allowed to ship them off to their grandparents until the end of the lockdown?"

I chuckle. "Probably not."

"Shame." He sighs and sips his tea. "You seem to be doing better this week. Getting on top of things?"

I nod. "Getting there, I think. I lost a big commission last week, but it's taken a bit of the pressure off." I usually find a bit of pressure good for motivation, but this time, having more breathing room on my deadlines has, surprisingly, improved my productivity. Or the two things are unrelated.

"I know what you mean. Now I'm not working, I've been able to help these two a bit more. Leon's stuff is straightforward enough, but Mia's seems needlessly complicated. Even I don't get half of it."

I know Mia is still at junior school, and I find myself wondering whether the teachers are overcompensating, trying to prove something. Every now and then I am a teensy bit grateful I don't have to deal with all that. "Well, if there's anything I can help with, I owe you."

He laughs. "Want to adopt them?"

I close my eyes and shake my head. I don't know if he realises that hurts. It's just a sarcastic comment to him, but to me, it sounds like he'd give away something I wish I had.

"No, but you can borrow my tent if you like. It's in the shed. Put it up in your garden and they can camp out for a couple of nights. Give you the house to yourself."

His eyes widen and he glances over his shoulder at the shed. "You're a genius."

"You're welcome."

Day 34

The weather has been bleak this week, raining on and off. Amanda and I have missed two messages in a row, and I'm suffering from withdrawal. That's my daily pick-me-up, and I need it.

Tawny has disappeared this morning though, so I'm hopeful. I kind of want a chance to tell Amanda about how my commissions are progressing this week. Actually, I want to tell her I'm doing better full stop.

When Tawny returns, she's wearing something made of fabric like a bandana around her neck. I manage to catch her and take it off. It's a facemask. It's pale grey cotton and has a cat's nose, mouth and whiskers drawn on it with fabric paint.

> *Hey Nick, missed you. Made you a present for when things ease up. Hope you like it.*
>
> *— A*

I love it. I think I love the idea that she missed me even more.

Day 36

I'm losing our game of Hangman! The gallows have been assembled, the noose lowered, and my man only needs two arms, then he's dead. Tawny has been no help.

Amanda gave me a clue: *Movie / Wish I was here.*

$$\_ E D D \_ A \_ O \_$$

I've already eliminated the other vowels plus S, T, H, M, L and W. Only got the D on my last guess.

I'm feeling semi-confident about R, but if that's not right I'm down to my last life. This is nerve-racking.

I go with R. Now I have to wait till tomorrow to know if I'm right and, as with every message, I get that feeling of it not being enough. I made a promise to myself; no matter how much I think she might welcome it, I will not send her any contact details until she asks or sends me hers. I am sticking to that promise. I will not be led into temptation by a game of Hangman.

Day 37

R E D D R A _ O _

Well now it's obvious, isn't it! I fill in the rest of the letters, G and N. Movie and "wish I was here" because our local pub is the Red Dragon. I feel kind of stupid for not seeing it earlier.

I could murder a proper pint. I blame Amanda for getting me thinking about the pub. I tell her this.

Day 38

The sun's come out today, and it's bloody lovely outside. I'm sitting on my patio with a lovely cup of tea, and I'm wearing my shorts again. Amanda tells me that more sunlight and vitamin D might improve my mood. Part of me likes to think she's trying to trick me into getting my kit off, but shorts is all she's getting unless she wants Carol next door to complain to the council again.

I might even hang some laundry outside today. It gives me an incentive to do it.

I'm feeling so much better this week. Maybe I'm starting to get the hang of this new normal. I'm sleeping better, less erratically, since I started forcing myself to go to bed by eleven. I've cut down on... self-soothing. I've been exercising every other day.

The trick has been setting smaller goals. What Amanda said about not expecting myself to be at my best has stuck with me. Now I'm aiming for and achieving 75% rather than beating myself up for not doing 120%.

I even got two, yes TWO, commissions finished and out the door yesterday afternoon. One I'd been avoiding from earlier in the month, but once I worked through the mental block, I was damn proud of the result.

A little bit of accomplishment has gone a long way towards lifting my mood, and I've decided I need more.

While I sip my tea, I browse through job posts on the freelance sites I use and pick a few to apply for. I prefer illustration, but graphic design gigs help pay the bills – quick and easy commissions for small businesses who need social distancing posters, new opening hours, take out menus for restaurants that haven't done take out before. There's loads of work around if you're quick.

There's a scrabble of claws at the end of the garden as Tawny climbs the fence from the footpath. She walks the line of the panel until she can jump onto the roof of the shed, then down onto the water butt and down again onto the grass with a soft thud.

"Nice nap?" I ask. I try to contain the excitement I experience each morning in anticipation of Amanda's reply. It can be tricky to catch Tawny if I spook her and she decides I'm "being weird". I have to wait, play it cool.

She rubs her chin on the corner of the shed and scratches it to confirm it is still hers, then trots across the lawn. I put my hand down to call her over. She seems mildly confused by my being outside, as if I am an indoor piece of furniture out of place.

But it doesn't faze her for long. She jumps up on the garden table for a fuss. She gets her cuddles, and I get my mail.

On one side Amanda has drawn a doodle of an empty gallows and a freed stick figure holding a scroll of paper with the word "pardon". It's cute. The message on the other side reads:

Correct. And sorry! Fancy a drink together when all this is over? P.S. Wash your hands. It's probably nothing but I felt a bit feverish this morning.

— A

A drink together? Does that mean I'm not the only one feeling some kind of connection here? I mean, the other little flirty messages could have been kidding around, but this sounds like she'd genuinely be interested in meeting me. It's getting hard to deny that I have feelings for her, even though we've never met. I hope she's pretty. I don't mean that in a superficial, pre-defined standard way, I just mean that I hope that, whatever she looks like, I feel an attraction.

The warm rush of excitement and hope is all mashed up with stomach-churning dread as I re-read her message. Feverish. I pull the cat closer for the comfort of her soft little body and press my cheek to her fur. I hate this pandemic. I don't want Amanda to get sick. It could kill her.

Day 39

Yesterday, after I'd let my fear and frustration fade, I went up to my office and drew Amanda a sketch. She knows I'm an artist – it's come up in our conversation several times – but until she sent me that doodle, the thought of sending her one of my drawings hadn't occurred to me. Funny really.

I drew a sleeping Tawny on a tabletop beside two pints and an unfurled note like the ones we've been exchanging that read: *It's a date.*

I hope that's what she has in mind. On the other side, I wrote in my tiniest handwriting:

Amanda, I want you to know that your messages have helped get me through a really tough time. Your words put a smile on my face even on my darkest days. I would love to meet you and spend some time with you. We could work something out if you don't want to wait, but it's your choice.

– N

I waited until this morning to pop the note in the holder on Tawny's collar (I snuck it in while she was having her breakfast). If I'd done it yesterday, I would have been tempted to chicken out each time I saw it still there as Tawny went about her day.

Tawny's out now. It's too late to take it back. But at least I won't have to wait long. God, I hope Amanda feels the same.

The cat comes home at just gone eleven.

Amanda's message reads:

Me too! Nick, if you only knew what you've meant to me these past few weeks. But I'm so sorry, I have to stop writing. I was coughing all night. I don't want to risk infecting you. I'll write again when it's safe. Don't go anywhere.

—A

"Shit." My chest tightens and my voice cracks even on that one word. How?! Neither of us has been anywhere to get infected. What are the chances that she picked it up off some item from the shops her parents dropped off, or a parcel from the postman? We've both been so careful, I know we have.

I run up to my bathroom and scrub my hands. Count to 20. Rinse. They're shaking. I'm wheezing a bit and take two deep puffs on my inhaler. It's okay. She's sensible. She knows to seek help immediately. That's probably all she means anyway – that she'll be at the hospital getting treated.

In my office, I write my reply. I'm sending her my number. I know I said I wouldn't but those rules don't apply now that we've... it's not the same. I have to know she's okay. I wish I could somehow order Tawny to make a second trip today, but I know she won't. I'll have to be patient because I'm not going to go looking for her house – that's a line I won't cross, just in case I'm wrong and I've read things into her words that aren't there.

The note sits in the holder taunting me all day. To help take my mind off it, I read through all of Amanda's previous messages, and it hits me.

The hospital. She went to the hospital about three weeks ago.

I hope she calls.

Day 40

There's no message today. My note is gone from the holder, but Amanda hasn't replied. Or called.

I'm worried.

I send her another note, begging her to let me know she's okay.

DAY 41

My note from yesterday is still there. She hasn't called.

I call the hospitals with her first name and postcode. That's all I know about her. They can't find any record that she's been admitted.

Now I'm panicking.

It's raining, so maybe Tawny hasn't made her visit today. It wouldn't be the only day we've missed in the last month because our message delivery system hasn't felt like going out. But it wasn't raining earlier at her usual nap time. And besides, I know yesterday's message got through. Amanda has my number. She could text me to let me know how she is.

Unless she can't for some reason. I don't even entertain the thought that she might not want to.

I pace my kitchen, staring out into the garden. Am I blowing this out of proportion? Amanda's not reckless. She'd know to call for help the moment she got sick. She knows her body won't be able to fight it off.

But there are a million reasons something might go wrong. My mind fills with worst-case scenarios. What if they're over capacity and can't get to her? What if there's some misunderstanding about her condition and they tell her to wait and see for a couple of days. What if...

"Screw it," I mutter, grabbing my coat and shoes.

I don't even lock the patio doors behind me, I just squelch my way across the lawn to the gate at the bottom of the garden. It takes me a moment to open the combination padlock; it's so rare I go this way, and my hands are trembling.

The path is full of puddles, but the gravel under the top layer of mud is firm. I work my way to the left, spying through knot holes or hoisting myself up to peer over the fences of each property.

At the first conservatory I find (number 18, I think), I try the gate; it won't open. When I scramble up, I see it's just a bolt a third of the way down, not a lock, and with some cursing and bruised abs from draping myself over the wood, I manage to open it.

There's an open window in the conservatory – left that way for a cat to climb through, perhaps? But that's not proof this is the right house.

I knock. I wait. There's no answer. The worsening rain soaks my jeans under the hem of my jacket and drips down my face.

In the conservatory there's a wicker three-piece suit – a two-seater and two armchairs. On the two-seater, there's a scrunched-up blanket with a Tawny-sized depression in the centre.

"Amanda?" I call at the open conservatory window. There's no response. "Amanda? It's Nick."

I don't know what to do. Should I assume the worst and call an ambulance? Isn't it more likely she's already gone to hospital, and the administrators I spoke to just couldn't (or wouldn't) identify her from the scant information I had?

The only other possibility is that she hasn't been able to call for help for some reason, and she's in there, dying.

There's a muffled crash, like a vase falling on the floor or something. Upstairs.

I'm going in.

I try the doors, just in case, but they're locked, so I scramble in through the window. It's a tight squeeze (I think I've put on a bit of weight during lockdown). I fall in a heap on the floor inside, knocking an armchair sideways. I take a moment to rub the bruises. My chest is tight. I take a puff on my inhaler, so I can catch my breath and find my feet.

The internal door into the kitchen opens when I try the handle. "Amanda? It's Nick. I'm coming in, okay?"

There's no response, but I don't expect there to be. I shed my dripping jacket and muddy shoes and leave them on the mat in the conservatory.

As I venture further in, that gut feeling of breaking the rules returns tenfold. What I am doing right now, being in another person's house, is illegal. I mean, technically breaking in has always been illegal, but that's not what I mean. I'm breaking *lockdown*.

Rainbow knitting. Photon League issue one on the coffee table. Now I'm sure I'm in the right place.

Forefront in my mind is the knowledge that I am also an "at-risk" person. I haven't forgotten I'm supposed to be isolating for my own safety, and that deliberate contact with someone who is infected is bloody stupid, but it's an emergency. Amanda is in a much higher category of "at-risk" than I am. My lungs might be shit, but I have an immune system that can fight the virus. She doesn't.

Is there even a way she *can* survive? If they take her off the immunosuppressants so her body can fight the virus, won't that mean her body will reject her transplant? I wish I'd asked what the transplant was. I mean, if it's a kidney, maybe they could put her on dialysis and get her a new one. If it's a heart then...

I can't. I can't think that far ahead.

I find the stairs, head up.

She's lying on her bed in the largest of the three bedrooms, staring up at the ceiling, breath shallow. I pause in the doorway. I've never seen her before, but I know it's her. Her skin is washed out pale, and her hazel eyes are scared and full of tears. She's so small, except she's not; it's a trick of perspective. There's a lamp and a book on the floor as if she pushed them off to get my attention. I'm feeling so many conflicting things I can't separate them.

"Amanda," I move towards her.

"Can't breathe," she gasps, almost too quiet and raspy to hear. It sets her coughing, and I'm terrified that she might die right here and now.

Without stopping to acknowledge how risky it could be for me, I join her on the bed and help her sit. I hold her until the coughing subsides, rubbing her back in slow circles. There's a wet sound to her breathing, and I know it's very serious.

"It's okay," I murmur, stroking her hair. "I'm here. You're going to be okay." With my other hand, I take my inhaler out of my pocket, shake it, and hold it to her lips. I don't know if it will help, but steroids treat inflammation, right? It's worth a try, and I don't think it can make it worse. "On three." We count; she inhales. "And again." She takes another dose.

It doesn't have much effect at first. She clings to me as I dial 999 on my mobile. I feel her fear like it's my own.

We wait for the ambulance. In the time it takes to arrive, she becomes a part of me. I don't know if she feels the same, but I want to believe she does. She can't speak, but her breathing seems to ease a little. She looks up into my eyes and grips my sleeve like she's afraid I'll let go.

I hold her gaze. "Everything's going to be okay. There's too much we still have to say to each other, so it has to be, yeah?"

Tears fall from her eyes as she nods. I kiss her forehead, hold her to me. I don't ever want to let her go.

But, when the ambulance arrives, I have to.
They take her away. They take a part of me away.
I'm not allowed to go with her.

Day 42

I didn't sleep a wink last night.

I don't know what do to with myself.

Day 45

Dave has just dropped off my groceries, and I've told him everything. He's sitting at my garden table, shock painted across his features. I'm standing inside the patio doors, which are cracked open barely enough for us to hear each other because I'm terrified I could now be carrying the virus.

All I've heard about Amanda is that she's in intensive care. I got a call from her mum yesterday to thank and update me, but her mum and I are complete strangers, so it was stilted and a bit weird.

"This is like some crazy rom-com shit," Dave says, shaking his head.

I would agree if it wasn't for the fact that the woman I think I might be falling for will probably die from this evil virus, and there's not a damn thing I can do. I can't even go to the hospital and hold her hand. It's not a comedy, it's a tragedy. I don't say this to Dave. I just smile and nod.

"She'll be fine," he says, more seriously. "The

doctor's will sort her out. You just concentrate on staying healthy. You look like shit. Are you sleeping? Eating?"

"Trying to," I say, my voice downbeat.

"Is there anything I can do?"

"Nah, mate, you've done loads." And I mean it. Dave and Amanda have had an equal hand in keeping me alive and sane, and I owe them both so much.

"Right, well, take care, okay?" He gets up from the patio chair. "And call me, yeah? You know Chelle and I are here for you."

"Thanks, mate." It means a lot.

My friend leaves, and I am alone with my thoughts again. I'm knackered, but I need to keep going. I'm not the one in hospital, so my life isn't on hold, even though I feel like it should be. I ferry the groceries in, pack them away and scrub my hands. Count to 20. Rinse. Then I trudge up to my office to try and find a scrap of focus and get some work done. Everything is uphill.

DAY 46

I can't do this.

I've contacted all my current clients to explain the situation and that my work may be delayed. My head is in a dark place, and I can't give them the attention they need right now. They've all been amazingly understanding and supportive, and I've promised myself I'll make it up to them in the long run.

I got my actual sketchbooks out for the first time in a while, and I've been trying to use my drawing to process all the noise in my head. Some of what I started throwing out on the pages seemed to flow together, so now I'm approaching it as a comic. It's been a long, long time since I've "written" my own script, but maybe it's what I need right now.

Day 50

I'm supposed to go and get tested today. I've got to drive to the health centre and back. It's been weeks since I've driven anywhere. I wonder if it will feel weird.

As I change into some jeans to venture outside, my mind is on Amanda. It's always on her. I sent her mum a text three days ago. All she replied was: *No change. Sorry.* I'm not sure how often it would be acceptable to contact her, and so I'm trying not to. I'm sure she's busy updating family and Amanda's real friends. I'm not sure where I fit into her life. Do I fit at all? I know where I *want* to fit, where I *feel* like I *should* fit, but in reality, I'm just a neighbour whose cat has boundary issues.

I wash my hands (count to 20, rinse), pocket the facemask that Amanda made me, and head out to find out if I'm dying too.

It feels alien and a bit scary going out my front door for the first time in weeks.

I see more people than I thought I would.

They do know there's a pandemic happening, right?

Day 51

Covid-19 test results: *negative.*

By some miracle I didn't catch it from Amanda during that half an hour we waited for the ambulance. I feel guilty.

I wish I had it and she didn't. Hell, at this point I'd sign up for another round of cancer and chemo if it meant she lived.

Have they let anyone be with her at the hospital? What if there's no one with her and she dying, scared and alone?

If she dies, I won't get a chance to say goodbye.

Will anyone even tell me when it happens?

Does she think about me?

I think Tawny senses my melancholy. She keeps hanging around in the same room with me like she's keeping an eye on me. Every time I sit down, she wants lap cuddles. It's helping. It's helping a lot. But I don't think she appreciates me leaving her fur damp with tears.

Day 52

It's early evening, and I'm sat at the kitchen table with my laptop. Bills for the end of April have come in, and my Internet banking tells me I'm overdrawn. I've been so shit at finding and delivering work on time since the lockdown started that I'm a bit short this month. I transfer some money from my savings. It's not like I'll need it for a holiday or anything this year.

I need to pull myself out of this latest rut. It's a deep one.

I'd felt like I was getting on top of things before Amanda got sick, but that's gone completely out the window. No, wait, that sounds like I blame her illness for my failings, and that's not what I mean at all. I think about it a lot, trying to figure out how I feel and why. I barely know her, and I should probably be able to put it out of my mind but I can't. I think... I think she's supposed to be part of my life, and if she dies now, we're never going to get to find out what our life together should have been. That thought haunts me.

All the life she's supposed to live is slipping away, and it's taking a part of mine with it.

It's very hard to get on with living when I feel like I'm not all here.

Tawny is pacing by the French doors, asking to be let out. She could use her cat flap, but she likes to remind me I'm her human slave occasionally.

I get up from the table to open the doors. I stay there, letting the breeze cool my face and my hot, puffy eyes.

My phone rings on the table. It's an unknown number, and I consider letting it go to voicemail since I am not in the mood to talk to strangers right now. But it's a mobile number, not a business number, so it could be a client. I owe them for their patience.

I pick it up and return to the door.

"Hello?"

"Nick?" asks the faint and raspy voice on the other end of the line.

"That's me. Who's this?"

"Guess who's off her ventilator?" Harsh coughs follow, but not continuously.

I grip the door frame, suddenly unsteady. "Amanda?"

"Hey."

For a moment I can't speak. My eyes fill with tears that cascade down my cheeks, and I struggle to breathe past the lump in my throat. The relief *hurts*. Everything I've been feeling, thinking, it all gushes out at once. I'm so overwhelmed I can't think.

"Nick?"

"I'm sorry. I'm here." I swipe the tears from my face with the back of my hand. "I'm just... I was so worried."

"Me too." She coughs again, harsher. Her breathing is laboured. She sounds weak.

"Should you be talking?"

"I'm not supposed to." A pause to cough again. "But I wanted to hear your voice."

I have to sit down as my chest tightens with emotion. I didn't imagine it. There is something between us. "Are you... is the worst over? You're going to be okay?"

"Yeah. I'm okay. They had to amputate my leg though."

I do a mental double-take, trying to remember whether that's supposed to make sense and drawing a blank. "What?"

"My bone graft failed. I'm actually okay with it. Weirdly."

She coughs again, and I feel bad for keeping her talking.

"Hey, listen. You need to rest. Text me, yeah?"

"Okay."

But I don't want to hang up. I want to keep this connection live, so I know she's still there. "You have to get better so we can go for that drink at the Dragon after all this is over. Remember?"

"I remember. I can't wait. I'll call when I can."

"Take it easy."

She hangs up. I clutch my phone in both hands, elbows on the table, forehead resting on my knuckles and just breathe. I'm not sure how long I sit there, but eventually Tawny jumps up on the table and headbutts my hands to protest that I haven't fed her. It's getting dark outside.

"Do you want your dinner?" My stomach rumbles too. "Let's both have some dinner."

Day 57

Knowing that Amanda is out of the woods has been like taking a suffocating bag off my head. I'm still worried about her. I'm still constantly thinking about what she's suffering through, and how much I wish I could be there to help in some way. But at least now I can sleep, eat, and generally function as a person. She texts me a few times a day. Mainly sardonic little comments like "still alive, but it's early." I love her sense of humour, but I'm not sure I appreciate it right now. So long as it helps her cope then it's good.

I've left all my bigger commissions on hold and picked up some simple graphic design gigs to tide me over financially. With Amanda so ill, I'm just not in a good place to be working on art to other people's specs.

I've made some progress with the comic I started. It's kind of dark and conceptual, but it's been helping me process.

In the last few days, I've been able to consider it a bit more critically, get a better sense of what it wants to be as a whole. I sent an outline and some pages to a publisher friend of mine this morning. He's just got back to me saying he loves it and wants to know when I can send more. So, that's a thing.

I'm expecting a call from my parents sometime today. I've been leaving my sister to deal with them and staying out of the drama, but Mum likes to phone once a fortnight to check in. I'm sketching some new pages at my desk when my phone rings. I answer without looking at the screen.

"Helloo."

"Hey, Nick."

It's not mum.

"Amanda?" The room does a slight tilt as if her voice has a magnetic effect on my blood. I mentally switch gears. "How are you feeling?"

"Much better." She sounds it too. Her voice is clearer, brighter. I can hear more energy in it, and I feel lighter for hearing it. "They're talking about keeping me in for another five or six days at the moment," she adds.

"What? And then you'll be—"

"Home, yeah."

There's a weight of expectation in those words that

I like. "That's good. I think Tawny misses you. Or she misses her naps in your conservatory, one or the other." I recline in my office chair.

"Is she the only one who misses me?"

I'm suddenly grinning so hard my face aches, and I'm glad no one can see me. "What do you think? Of course, I miss you. I was all ready to start our next game of Hangman."

She laughs. It's food for my soul.

"No, but seriously," I say, giving in to a deep need to unburden myself. "I do miss you. I know it might sound silly, but you mean a lot to me and I... I'm not sure one little message a day is going to be enough for me anymore."

"Me neither. I think about that moment when you found me. I think about it all the time. I was delirious for the first couple of days and I started to wonder whether I imagined it. Then I heard the doctors talking about... well, about how close it came. They were talking about you and the steroids you gave me, and I realised it was all real. You saved my life, Nick. How did you know I needed you?"

I let out a long breath, my throat constricting with emotion. "When you didn't call, I phoned the hospitals and they said you weren't there. I just... I don't know, I had to know you were okay. Why didn't you get help?"

"I tried. It just came on so fast. After I wrote you that last note, I phoned the 111 helpline and they said I should go to the hospital if I could make it there on my own, or to call for an ambulance if I started having trouble breathing."

"So why didn't you?" I ask, voice cracking because I'm reliving all the fear.

"I was going to, but I don't have a car. There's no taxi's running, no busses. I talked to my mum and dad on Monday evening. I couldn't risk infecting them, so we were going to get my brother Ben to come down to drive me, but he couldn't get here until Wednesday evening. I didn't feel too bad Tuesday morning. I mean, I was coughing, and I felt really ill, but not much worse than Monday, so I thought that would be okay. Then on Tuesday night it started getting worse, so I planned to call 111 again in the morning and have them come and get me. I went to sleep, but I woke up in the night and couldn't breathe. I couldn't even get downstairs to my phone. It felt like I was going to pass out every time I moved. I think I did black out a couple of times. I thought Ben would find me when he came to get me.

Only it wasn't him, it was you. And if you hadn't found me when you did, he might have found me dead."

I grip the arm of my chair, the frustration and fear welling up again. "You could have called *me*," I say, not in an accusatory tone, just one of desperation. Even though it's all over, my mind wants to change it so it played out differently.

"I know. And I thought about it. I did. But I was worried about making you sick. I thought if I called you, you might do something stupid. And I was probably right, wasn't I? Because you did something stupid anyway."

I huff. "Yeah, probably. But I'd do it again."

"It doesn't matter now. I know I should have called for an ambulance sooner, and that's on me. The important thing is I'm okay. And you're okay. And I know you'll be there for me when I get back."

My smile widens. "I'd like that." Then it hits me what she might mean. "Are we... are we starting something here? Like a... a relationship something?"

"Well, we could be waiting a while if our first date has to be after the lockdown," she says with a giggle. "So yes, Nick, I would like to start a relationship something with you."

My phone beeps, making my raw nerves jump. I hold it away from my ear to check the screen and see my mum's smiling face on the incoming call. "Bollocks."

Amanda makes an affronted "hmm".

"No, not you! My mother is calling. She has the worst timing. I need to answer this. Can I call you back in twenty minutes?"

"I'm not going anywhere," Amanda says.

"Okay, I won't be long. Bye."

I hang up and answer my mum's call. "Hey Mum, how are you?"

"Are you alright, Nicky? You sound out of breath."

"I'm fine." I take a quick puff on my inhaler and prompt her to tell me all the family gossip, drama and angst to get it off her chest (it's like draining a recurring cyst). She asks about Amanda – I'd mentioned my friend had been taken to hospital when she last called, so of course she remembered that. I update her and hint that Amanda *might* become more than a friend. She's giddy, and I'm worried she might start knitting baby booties as soon as she hangs up. I try to manage her expectations a bit, but on the inside, I'm giddy too.

Once I get Mum off the phone, I call Amanda back and we talk for forty more minutes about all sorts of things. When the conversation naturally swings in the right direction, I ask the second thing I've been dying to know (after why she didn't call for help).

"You said before they had to.. your leg?"

"Oh, right, yeah," she says with a sigh that sounds more embarrassed than anything.

Is she worried I'll be put off by her amputation? Because it doesn't bother me in the slightest.

"It's kind of a long story," she says.

"I've got nothing else to do right now."

She laughs and then launches into her tale. "It was a car accident. Nearly eight years ago now. My husband and I were driving on the motorway, and there was a lorry, and... it doesn't really matter how it happened. He didn't make it. I survived, but my right leg was crushed. There wasn't enough bone left to pin it, so they used a bone graft."

"Wait, wait, hang on... you're a widow?"

She sighs, full of sadness. "I am. But it's long enough ago now that I've been able to move on."

"I'm so sorry." It might seem like a weird thing to say, given my intentions towards her, but I wouldn't wish that on anyone. I'm never going to be jealous or resentful of a dead man, that's just not me.

"Thanks." There's a pause that neither of us rushes to fill, and Amanda takes a tight breath before she continues. "Anyway, the thing about bone grafts is that they're safe. Easy. It's just dead tissue they use for structure, and they get your body to grow onto it, not the other way around. It comes from a tissue bank. Like blood."

I settle in to listen because this is part of who she is but also because it's fascinating in its own right.

"Bone graft rejections are rare, but not unknown. Apparently I'm a one in a million case. Not long after the surgery, my body started to reject it. It wasn't particularly fast, though, so they put me on the immunosuppressants and it worked. For the best part of seven years, I've been running, skipping and jumping like I always did. And then a little bit before the pandemic kicked off, I started getting some pain in my shin. I was having some tests—"

"Is that why you were at the hospital last month?" I ask, putting the pieces together.

"Exactly. It was all a bit inconclusive, and they hadn't decided what to do. When I was taken in with Covid, they took me off the drugs. And, well, it turns out I had an infection around the graft, but the drugs were masking it. In the time it took for me to start to fight off the virus, it went nuts, and I nearly went septic. It was touch and go for a couple of days."

I catch myself clutching the armrest again. I don't like thinking about how close she came to not leaving that hospital.

"I wasn't strong enough for surgery," she continues, "and the infection had damaged my bone. I couldn't fight both the infection and the Covid. It was my leg or my life, so, chop chop."

"Hang on, if you weren't strong enough for surgery, how did they do the amputation?"

She chuckles darkly. "I was awake."

My stomach rolls. "No."

"Mmm-hmm. Epidural. Like for pregnancy. Numbs you from the waist down. Mostly."

"Nope," I say again, shaking my head. That's too vivid a picture.

"Couldn't risk a general anaesthetic, could they? So we did it proper barber-surgeon style. Bite down on a stick and be quick." She's deliberately winding me up now. "Do you want to know what a bone saw sounds like?"

"I do not," I say, swallowing another wave of

nausea.

She laughs again, clearly enjoying the fact she's making me squirm. "It's okay. It wasn't that bad, not really. Only took about ten minutes. And I feel like... I could have lost my leg in the accident, but I've had these extra seven years as a bonus. I'll get used to it."

"Yeah, you will." I somehow doubt it will slow her down at all.

"This has been really nice, Nick. Can we do it again?"

"Of course. Probably best if you call me, yeah?"

"Yeah, and do you have Facebook Messenger? It'd be cool just to chat sometimes. And, you know, play Hangman."

"I do. I'll text you a link."

We sign off and after taking a few minutes to pop downstairs and make a cup of tea, I get back to my sketches. For the first time in ages, I find myself fully absorbed by the work, and it feels great.

About two hours later, I get a message. It's a photo of my girl in her hospital bed, showing off her bandages and giving me two thumbs up and a cheesy grin. That's it, I'm done. She has me for life.

Day 64

I have a date!

Via Zoom.

They let Amanda come home yesterday. We've chatted a few times while she's been recovering in hospital, but there's been a certain lack of privacy. Making this an official "date" was her idea. Proposed via cat message this morning after Tawny visited to welcome her home. I'm so looking forward to it.

My kitchen table is dressed up with a tablecloth and candles, and I'm cooking. My laptop is set up across the table where she'd be sitting if we could do this properly.

I decided on salmon en-croûte with potato gratin and steamed veg. Mainly because that was the fanciest thing I had in the house, and I could hardly send Dave on an extra trip to the shops for date-night supplies. I check the carrots are soft, and the oven beeps to say everything should be ready. I plate up and shove mine in the oven to keep warm. Amanda's I cover with another plate and wrap with a tea towel, then I slip my shoes on and head down the garden to the gate, along the path and in at number 18. Amanda's gate isn't bolted this time.

She waves from inside the conservatory. Balanced on her crutches. The right leg of her leggings is turned up above the knee. Below the knee are bandages and air. It's only the second time I've seen her, and last time, she had two legs, but she looks a million times healthier and happier now. She's beautiful.

I hand her meal through the open window that Tawny uses to come and go.

"You got dressed up?" she says.

I cast a glance at my shirt and best jeans. "Only a little bit."

"You look nice."

I bask in the compliment like Tawny when she's found a patch of sunshine. "You too." God, I wish this lockdown was over, and I could just go in and spend time with her.

She looks down at the baggy t-shirt she's wearing as a dress, unconvinced. "What, in this? I didn't even put any makeup on."

I press my hand to the glass. "You look gorgeous."

She smiles, softly biting her lip. It makes my heart happy. I think I'm falling in love with her.

"Go on," she says, shooing me away with the hand holding her plate.

I walk backwards to the foot of her garden, wanting every glimpse I can get, then head home.

When I get home, she's video calling me. I answer before fetching my dinner, and we get settled.

"Wine?" I ask, holding up my bottle.

She shows me the bottle she has and we both pour.

"I haven't had a drink in seven years," she says. "Can you believe that? I wasn't supposed to with the drugs I was on. But now? I am going to enjoy this." She holds her glass out as if we can clink through the screen.

"Cheers."

"This looks amazing," she says, referring to the food. "And I am not just saying that because all I've had for three weeks is hospital food."

We eat. We talk. About the pandemic, about the Black Lives Matter protests, and about the other frightening things happening around the world. And about ourselves. Even though I'm slightly nervous, it's comfortable and easy. After everything we've been through, a first date holds no real fear. When we're done with the meal, Amanda suggests we relocate to our couches.

She asks me about my work.

"You're not supposed to talk about work on a date," I tease.

She puts on a mock-serious expression. "Oh, didn't you know? That doesn't apply to artists, writers and musicians. It's a well-established fact."

"Oh. No, I didn't get that memo."

"It's in the handbook, dummy."

"There's a handbook?" We're both laughing now. I haven't felt this good in so long.

She tsks, shaking her head. "Guys never read the handbook. It says you're permitted to ask about work if your boyfriend has some amazing creative talent."

I stare at her.

"What?" she teases, grinning.

Do I draw attention to the fact she called me her boyfriend, or do I just melt into a puddle without explanation? "Nothing," I say in a tiny voice.

The look she gives me says she knows exactly how whipped I am and she's fully okay with it. "So?" she says. "What have you been working on?"

I tell her about the comic I started while she was in hospital. About how dark and angsty it came out at first because I was using it as an outlet for everything I was feeling. As I tell her all this, I find everything I went through from the moment the ambulance took her away spilling out with it. Everything. The insomnia. Speaking to her mum. All the raw thoughts about not being an official part of her life and how cut-out I felt. Getting tested. Crying on my cat. The fact I've only been able to *function* since she first called and I knew she'd be okay.

It sets me crying again, and I try to wipe the tears away without her noticing. I don't want her to think I care more about myself than I do about her. What she went through was real, painful and terrifying; I was just lonely and worried.

She puts her hand out towards her screen. "It's okay," she says, softly. "I thought about you all the time too. About when you found me. When I was scared, I'd imagine you were with me, holding me like you did then."

"I wish I was with you right now."

"I know, me too," she says, gazing into her camera in a way that makes me feel like she's making eye contact.

I'm so tempted to break the rules right now, but I won't. One, that's not who I am, and two, we both know there's a chance she could still be contagious.

"They'll be time when it's over," she adds as if she can read my thoughts.

I sigh. "I know."

"It's so weird, isn't it?" she says. "We live so close to each other, but if we hadn't been isolating we might never have met. When we look back on this, that's what I'm going to remember."

Tawny chooses that moment to jump up on the sofa and walk on my laptop, somehow managing to minimise Amanda. She sniffs around, like she's searching for a lost kitten in distress, and does her "comfort the sad human" murp. Amanda laughs.

"I think she recognises your voice," I say, pulling the cat into my lap and bringing the screen back up.

"Of course, she does. And she wants the credit. Don't you girl? You did all the work. Our little matchmaker."

Tawny purrs.

Day 86

Once Amanda came home, it wasn't so hard to find my way back to a good equilibrium. I'm working again, but I'm not piling too much pressure on myself. I'm delivering on time and looking after myself. She's still recovering, obviously, but her check-up Covid test last week was negative, and her stump is healing well. It's not easy, but we're doing okay.

We've been dating for three weeks (four if you include that last week she was still in hospital before our first "date"). The closest we've been is two meters apart either side of my patio table like a scene from a Regency romance. But we talk every day and, well, there might have been some mutual "self-soothing" via FaceTime last night, once we'd researched it was encrypted.

She used the word "yearning" about me. I don't think anyone's ever *yearned* for me before. Not even my ex.

We're still sending cat messages, just for fun. Tawny thinks it's brilliant because she gets extra cuddles and Dreamies at Amanda's.

Pandemic wise, the country seems to be over the hump of this first wave, and this morning the government announced that adults who live alone may form a "support bubble" with another household. It basically means they are treated as the same household for the purposes of the lockdown and don't have to social distance. It specifically states that members of a bubble can enter and stay in each other's homes.

I just got a text from Amanda: *I want you in my bubble.*

Smirking to myself, I text back: *LOL. Is that a euphemism?*

She replies: *Hell yes. I'm coming over in 10mins. You better be ready.*

My stomach takes a swoop. Holy crap! Is this really happening? Now? I race upstairs to brush my teeth again and change out of my ratty joggers.

Nine minutes later I meet my girlfriend halfway across my lawn. She drops her crutches and throws her arms around my neck, and I catch her around the waist, holding her steady as she balances on her one foot. I breathe in her scent, feel the warmth of her body against mine, and the missing part of me that she's been carrying clicks back into place.

I think we're going to make it through the rest of this lockdown just fine.

Not everyone experienced the global events of 2020 the same way. Some lives were touched directly by the virus; many were lucky enough not to get sick or lose a loved one. Many watched the Black Lives Matter protests on the news; others saw them from inside the crowd. Some followed the rules; some thought the rules were stupid and shouldn't apply to them.

A lot of creative people processed 2020 through their art. I wrote this romance novelette. It was my way of documenting the lockdown experience – the way it affected me and the people around me – and trying to turn it into something sweet and uplifting.

You may or may not see your experience reflected in this book, but as Nick reflects when Dave explains about homeschooling and not finding time for intimacy with his wife, other people's struggles are different but no less valid. Whatever you struggled with, that's valid too.

After a lot of agonising over what to do with this story, I decided I wanted its uplifting message to be a positive thing *now*, while we're all still dealing with the pandemic and the troubles in the world. This meant making it available to as many people as possible, as soon as possible, as affordably as I could. If you've read and enjoyed the book, please recommend it to a friend.

ABOUT THE AUTHOR

Chrissey Harrison writes supernatural thrillers and other spec genre fiction. Books about monsters, magic, action and adventure, and fragile human characters trying to muddle through as best they can. She also writes occasional books and stories with no monsters or magic, and those she publishes as C. J. Harrison.

Her debut novel, *Mime*, released in July 2020, the first in her *Weird News* Series. Her short stories have featured in several anthologies, most recently *Forgotten Sidekicks* (Grimbold Books) and *Fire* (North Bristol Writers).

Chrissey is a science geek, crafter and fan of sci-fi, fantasy and horror. She lives in Clevedon, in a creaky old Victorian terrace with her partner, her 19 year-old goldfish Ambition, and tortoiseshell kittens Maple and Pecan.

THE STAR COIN PROPHECY

A time-travel romance novelette.

It's 2012. According to the Mayans the world is about to end… they might be right.

When local science reporter Ruth Anders attends a press conference for the Kepler project, she knows it's going to be a memorable experience but she never expects to be attacked by aliens from another world!

Zapped through time and space by a mysterious device, Ruth finds herself lost in the jungles of Central America and worse, it's 1959. Her only hope of getting back to her own time, and getting her quiet, safe life back, is explorer and archaeologist Neil Bell.

When the time comes though, will Ruth really want to go back to her old life?

Get a free eBook copy when you
subscribe to my newsletter.

Find out more at chrisseyharrison.com

MIME

Burning with no flames.
A gunshot with no bullet.

There's a supernatural killer on the loose...

Journalist Elliot Cross didn't believe in monsters. Not until his brother died at the hands of something unnatural.

Four years later, a string of impossible deaths leave the police baffled. Could this be Elliot's chance to make a difference? Enlisting the help of his (only) employee, Samantha, he quickly identifies the culprit – a demonic mime artist whose invisible creations are fatally real.

Way out of their depth, the search for a way to defeat the demon will take Elliot and Sam across the country, uncovering lost history, buried secrets, and a few new truths about themselves.

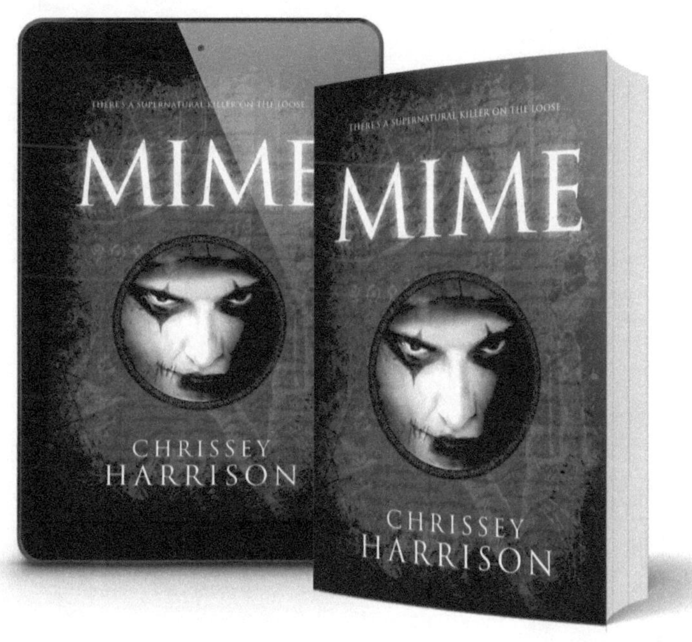

A supernatural thiller with a compelling mix of action and heart.

Find out more at

chrisseyharrison.com/mime